Kiona the Gardenian
Richard Haslam

YIN-LUNG DYNASTY
KATALEF
THE NORTHERN ISLES
URCALEDON
FALLOE
THE EMERALDS (YIN-LUNG DYNASTY)
SARDENIA
AUSTRIN
AFALLON
MERIDIAN SEA
CELESTE
ELY
NORTHERN ROMAN EMPIRE
LUSO
CASTELLAN
CORNEL
TOVI
ADSILA
THE GREAT WESTERN TRIBES
NEUTRAL TERRITORY
TETHYS SEA
YIN-LUNG DYNASTY
THE GREAT WATERS
THE TE
(DISPUT BETWEEN ROMA YIN-LU
THE GREAT WESTERN LANDS
THE MIGHTY WATERS
NORTHERN ROMAN EMPIRE
(FORMALLY IZTAX EMPIRE)

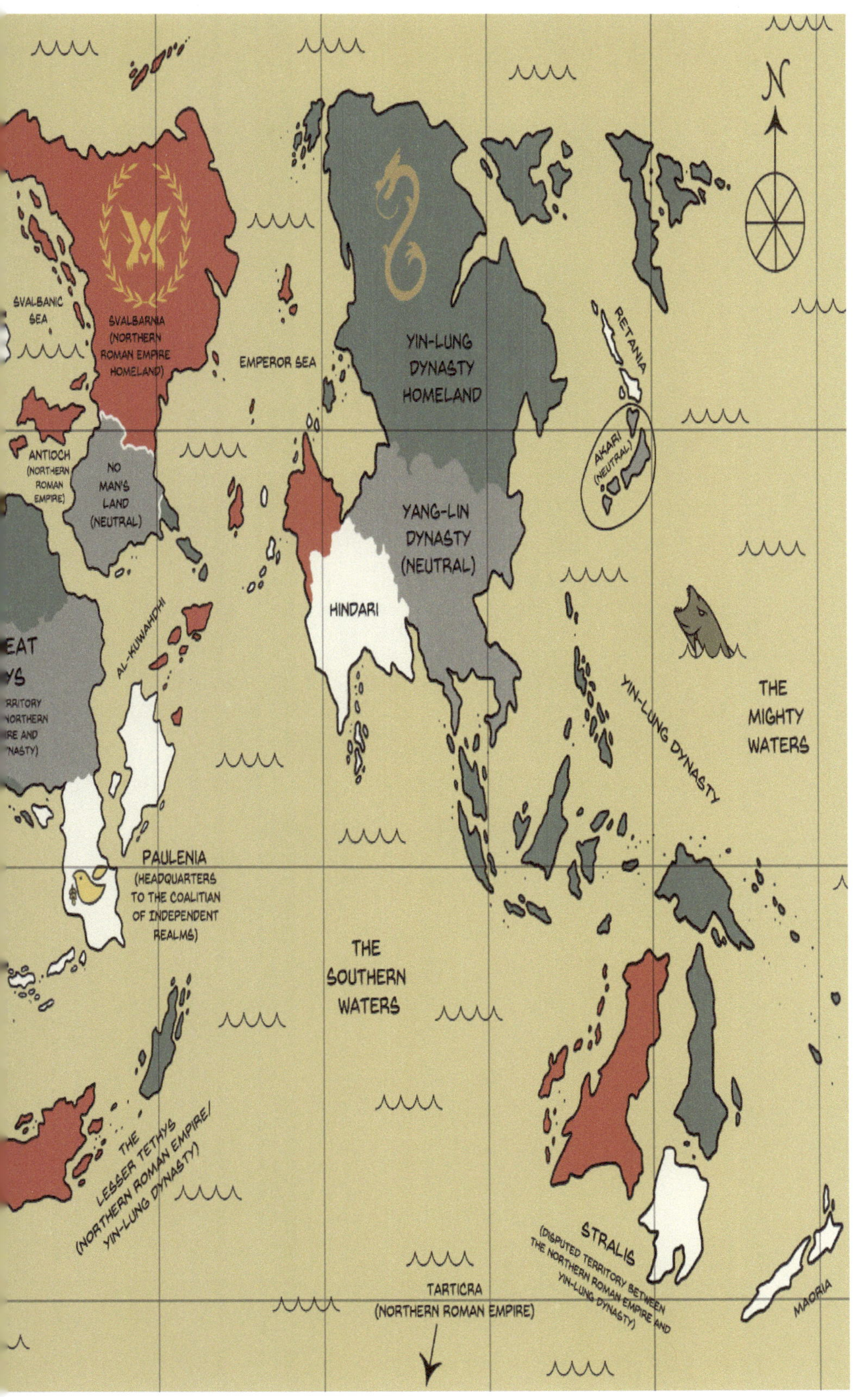

SVALBANIC SEA
SVALBARNIA (NORTHERN ROMAN EMPIRE HOMELAND)
EMPEROR SEA
YIN-LUNG DYNASTY HOMELAND
RETANIA
N
ANTIOCH (NORTHERN ROMAN EMPIRE)
NO MAN'S LAND (NEUTRAL)
YANG-LIN DYNASTY (NEUTRAL)
AKARI (NEUTRAL)
AL-KUWAHDHI
EAT YS
RRITORY ORTHERN IRE AND NASTY)
HINDARI
THE MIGHTY WATERS
YIN-LUNG DYNASTY
PAULENIA (HEADQUARTERS TO THE COALITIAN OF INDEPENDENT REALMS)
THE SOUTHERN WATERS
THE LESSER TETHYS (NORTHERN ROMAN EMPIRE/ YIN-LUNG DYNASTY)
STRALIS (DISPUTED TERRITORY BETWEEN THE NORTHERN ROMAN EMPIRE AND YIN-LUNG DYNASTY)
MAORIA
TARTICRA (NORTHERN ROMAN EMPIRE)

First Edition published in 2020, Second Edition Published in 2022, Third Edition Published in 2024, Fourth Edition Published in 2025, Fifth Edition Published in 2026

Written and Illustrated by Richard Haslam

Edited and Proofread by Jaris Ash

Independently Published

ISBN: 978-1-7384936-0-9

www.youarenow-here.co.uk

Dramatis Personae

<u>**The Main Cast**</u>

Kiona Atalanta Woodfall-Mac-Duff **Tiqvah**	Female Agender Female	The Forest Ringmaster in Gardenia's Trials of Maturity, and The Maid of The Heart. She is an angelic being (Virtue) incarnated, called **Tiqvah**, who represents Hope.	 
Levtiqvah **Levtiqvah – Tzila**	Agender Male Agender Female	Tiqvah's little brother and Heart Angel (Throne), who can understand the hearts of women and can take the form of women such as  **Okasa**,  **Shai**,  **Ailsa**, and **Megan**  	 

Achak Levi Woodfall-Mac-Duff *(Formerly)*	Male	Levtiqvah also has a Basis feminine form called **Levtiqvah-Tzila** and was formerly incarnated as Kiona's little brother, **Achak Levi Woodfall-MacDuff**.	
Rubecula Sander	Female	Kiona's platonic partner from another world and an old friend of the deceased Mira Melsbach; Levtiqvah's friend when in the form of Okasa.	
Nascha	Female	The Shikoba Tribe's chief's daughter from The Great Western Lands, who is Chilli-Tolerant and was arranged to marry Achak when he was the right age.	

Recurring Characters

Serena	Female	An English relic who survived "The Firestorm" via a coma, an old friend of Kiona and her parents.	

Abigail	Female	Kiona's friend from The Father's Chosen People with incredible speed and technical skills, royal guard to Princess Roso.	
Abenanka	Female	Kiona's childhood Ainu friend from Retania, who occasionally visits.	
Rui-Lin	Female	Abenanka's small friend from Retania with incredible strength. She is a refugee from the Yin-Lung Dynasty.	
Zoe	Female	Serena's best friend, whom she met once she recovered from her coma. She is from the floating island of Ariel.	
Toulouse	Female	Abigail's old friend, whose real name is **Tabitha.** She is skilled in the jousting-skating sport called 'Joutes de Patinage.'	
Jabari	Male	Zoe's brother from Ariel, who serves The Coalition.	

Name	Gender	Description
Gwendolyn	Female	A Cymru relic with a strong ancestral lineage, an old friend of Kiona's parents, and Achak's godmother.
Trevor	Male	Gwendolyn's relation and commander of their Britannic Legion.
Isonash	Male	An Ainu and an old friend of Abenanka and Rui-Lin from Retania.
Hasinaw	Female	Isonash's twin sister from Retania, her alias is **The Masked Piper**, who protects the vulnerable from injustice. She dwells with her family in Austrinia.
Birtá	Female	Isonash's Sámi wife.
Beartu	Male	Birtá's twin brother and Isonash's brother-in-law.

Mira Melsbach	Female	A deceased old friend of Kiona's parents. She later befriends Rubecula in her own world. She loved Levtiqvah in the form of Okasa.	
Freida Melsbach	Female	Mira's mother, who is of Austrinian origin. She resides in Saintmere.	
Wohali	Male	The Tree Inspector in Shenandoah.	
Francisco Cortes	Male	Commander of the Spanish Guard from Castellan.	
Angelica	Female	Supporter of The Coalition and rightful ruler of Svalbarnia.	
Svetlana	Female	Angelica's bodyguard.	

Saga Saul	Male	Supporter of Angelica's claim to Svalbarnia.	
Chronicle Sorcha	Female	Scottish Relic and an old friend to Kiona and her parents, right-hand to Saga Saul.	
Saga Cora	Female	High-ranking commander within The Coalition.	
Monedue	Male	Saga Cora's little brother. Mysterious and highly intelligent with his inventing skills.	
General Broadside	Male	An Emeralds general to the Gardenian-Free-Force, alias to **Finbar O'Conner**, Champion of the Gardenian Trials of Maturity.	
Atsila	Female	General Broadside's next-in-command, old friend to Kiona's mother, and Kiona's godmother.	

Name	Gender	Description	
Wayra	Male	The Meadow Ringmaster in Gardenia's Trials of Maturity.	
Helaku	Male	The Wold Ringmaster in Gardenia's Trials of Maturity. His real name is **Ferdinand**.	
Bornbazine	Male	Former Tundra Ringmaster in Gardenia's Trials of Maturity.	
Kaniehtiio	Female	Current Tundra Ringmaster in Gardenia's Trials of Maturity and Bornbazine's granddaughter.	
Greville	Male	The strongest and brawniest member of The Three Pillars in Gardenia's Trials of Maturity.	
Cairoli	Female	The fun-loving Jester member of The Three Pillars in Gardenia's Trials of Maturity.	
Loxley	Female	The stealthy and hidden member of The Three Pillars in Gardenia's Trials of Maturity.	

Hurenitay	Female	The Cuk (Autumn) Ringmaster in Retania's Trials of Maturity and formerly Isonash's girlfriend.	
Satoshi	Male	An Akari-Retanian who is an old friend of Isonash and the current boyfriend of Hurenitay.	
Rhoda Mac-Leod	Female	A shy Scottish girl who serves The Coalition.	

The Father's Angels

Hokmah	Agender Female	The Virtue angel that represents Wisdom.	
Hevel	Agender Male	The Virtue angel that represents Doubts.	
Savlanut	Agender Female	The Virtue angel that represents Patience.	

Talako Woodfall	Male	Kiona's deceased father. Former Forest Ringmaster in Gardenia's Trials of Maturity.	
Nakoma Amelia Woodfall-McDuff	Female	Kiona's deceased mother.	
Enid Woodfall	Female	Kiona's grandmother and mother to Kiona's father and Chief Samoset.	
Chief Samoset Woodfall	Male	Kiona's uncle on her father's side, brother to her father, and Chief of Shenandoah.	
Ahyoka Woodfall	Female	Chief Samoset's wife and Kiona's aunt on her father's side.	
Kwahu Woodfall	Male	Chief Samoset and Ahyoka's son and cousin to Kiona.	

Name	Gender	Description
Macha Woodfall	Female	Chief Samoset and Ahyoka's daughter and cousin to Kiona.
Calum Mac-Duff	Male	Kiona's grandfather and father of Kiona's mother.
Guise Mac-Duff	Female	Kiona's aunt and Kiona's mother's sister.
François D'Marmande MacDuff	Male	Kiona's French uncle and husband to Guise.
Evander MacDuff	Male	Guise and François D'Marmande's first son and Kiona's cousin.
Glen Mac-Duff	Male	Guise and François D'Marmande's second son and Kiona's cousin.
Joan Mac-Duff	Female	Guise and François D'Marmande's only daughter and Kiona's cousin.

Douglas Mac-Duff	Males	Guise and François D'Marmande's triplet son and cousin to Kiona.	
Yarrow Mac-Duff	Male	Guise and François D'Marmande's triplet son and cousin to Kiona.	
Lostock Mac-Duff	Male	Guise and François D'Marmande's triplet son and cousin to Kiona.	
Archibald MacDuff	Male	Kiona's mother's brother and Kiona's uncle.	
Chloe Mac-Duff	Female	Archibald's knowledgeable daughter and Kiona's cousin.	
Christie Mac-Duff	Male	A cardinal of the "Pre-Firestorm" faith and Kiona's cousin.	
Angus Mac-Duff	Male	Kiona's uncle.	

Robert Mac-Duff	Male	Angus's son and Kiona's cousin.	

<u>The Monarchy</u>

Princess Roso	Female	Charitable ruler of the Principality of Tovaro, and close friend to Kiona.	
Beatrix	Female	Princess Roso's young aunt, who is eight years older than her and protector.	
King Arthur IV	Male	Ruler of the Kingdom of Gardenia, related to Gwendolyn and Trevor.	
Queen Eurydice	Female	King Arthur IV's wife and co-ruler of Gardenia, older sister to Princess Roso.	
King Gordon IV	Male	Princess Roso and Queen Eurydice's father and Beatrix's brother, ruler of the Kingdom of Elyon.	

Queen Marieanne	Female	Spoilt and pampered ruler of the Kingdom of the Ur Alliance.	
Charles	Male	Queen Marieanne's eldest brother.	

The Yin-Lung Dynasty (Dragoons)

Yin Gui-Wu	Agender Male	Ruler of the Yin-Lung Dynasty, alias to his true identity as a Watcher, **Abraxas**.	
General Lao-Hu	Male	An Auspicious General who is cladded in thick armour and resembles a tiger.	
General Tang-Lang	Female	A stern general with sharp whips to resemble a Mantis.	

General Xie-Zi	Female	A subtle but stealthy general who takes many disguises, such as **Leiura**. She is known to strike like a scorpion.	
General Gui	Male	An Auspicious General known for his brute strength and size, with armour resembling a tortoise.	

The Northern Roman Empire (Aquilas)

Cynthia Caesar	Female	Ruler of the Northern Roman Empire, tyrannical older sister to Angelica.	
General Glandar	Female	Head of the Tenth Legion, Saga Cora's and Monedue's eldest sister.	

Commander Marcus	Male	Commander of the Tenth Legion.	
Commander Rufina	Female	Commander of the Tenth Legion.	
General Jauderell Banks	Male	Head of the Twelfth Legion.	
Commander Doncaster	Female	Commander of the Twelfth Legion.	
Commander Crewe	Female	Doncaster's little sister and commander of the Twelfth Legion.	

Antagonist

Granada Valentina	Female	Notorious criminal mastermind who preys around the Iberian Peninsula and originated from Frenchcornwall, Gardenia.	

The Revolutionaries of the Ur Alliance

Wallace Brunel	Male	Supreme Leader.	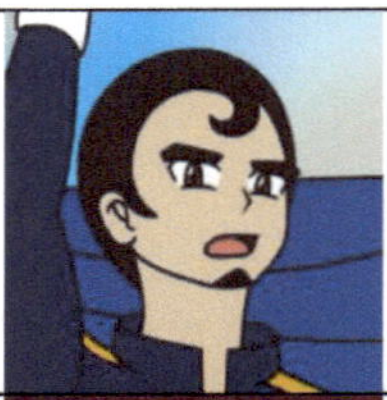
Benoît Mac-Leod	Male	Second in Com-mand.	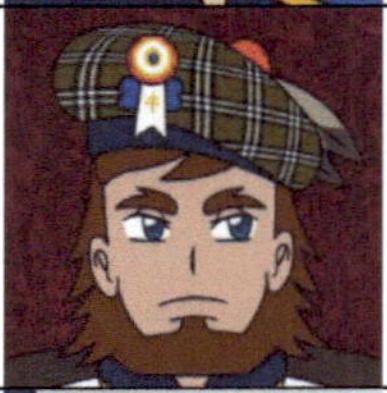
Clair Duval	Female	Commander, and an old friend of Kiona.	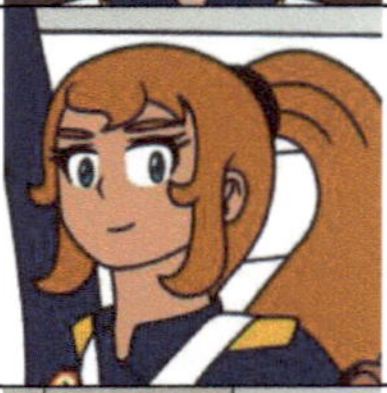
Alexander Phélippeaux	Male	Clair's second in command.	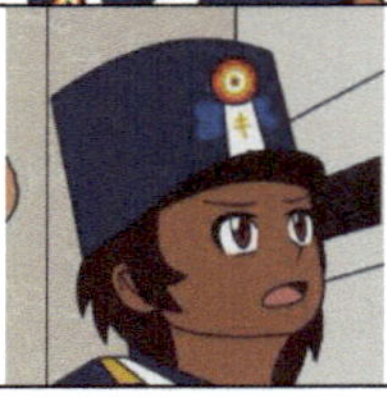

The Angellites

Eresh Kigal	Agender Female	A Fallen Angel who's originally called **Samael** (Agender Male), whose ambitions are the annihilation of humanity and all forms of leadership.	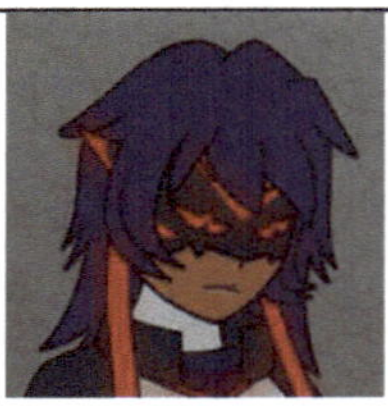

Keras	Agender Male	A firm but calm supporter of Eresh Kigal's shared goals.	
Elafiou	Agender Female	An ambitious supporter of the shared goals of Eresh Kigal.	

CONTENTS

The Eve of the Heart

The Retanian Twins

The Eve of the Heart
Sunday, 19th September 332
(1734)

The Journey

Twilight glinted for that short frame of the day within the vast and dense Forest Territory as Kiona, a Gardenian from the town of Shenandoah, was travelling eastwards through trees that were getting ready for the long, cold nights ahead, passing the hidden stone structures that were overgrown and somehow possessing a sort of familiar likeness in the fading light.

Ancient bones, like sticks, blended well beneath the fallen leaves and tangled tree roots, as if some burial mounds had been pushed upwards by the long passages of time. Beginning to get hungry, the hunting instinct of her ancestors kicked in, so, wearing her leaf-like cloak and being armed with crossbows on her gauntlets, Kiona stealthily snuck up and sniped a long-eared fanglop which had been busy feasting on a bird it had brought down. After skinning and gutting her catch, she lit a friendly fire on which to cook her meal, and before long, she was tucking into the tender meat.

As she was finishing off the last piece of flesh from the thighbone, the green stones on her crossbows that were vital for the sniping and fire began to flash rapidly in an alarming way. Understanding what it meant, she damped down the fire and quickly jumped into a hollow oak before it shuttered its door-like lid.

A while later, as Kiona was getting ready to sleep, a tremendous storm surged across the forest. This storm had an unnatural feel, and it was fortunate for Kiona that she was within the safety of the hollow oak; for if anyone were to be caught within its violence, then that poor person would most likely die from just breathing the air in, or, if that person somehow managed to survive through it, suffer a long and painful death. That is why this is called a curse storm.

As the sound of tinny and crackling thunder echoed outside, it did not deter Kiona's concerns and determination as she rested her head on the soft bed of leaves.

The air regained its freshness by the following morning. Long after the curse storm had passed and, after catching another fanglop for breakfast, Kiona continued her journey with her heart filled with courage and her faith set on her main goal. After carefully passing through a hidden glade where a leaf-horned eyetler grazed, she stumbled across a broad, muddy trackway that improved her navigation.

Not long after she began following the trackway, did she felt a slight tremor in the ground. That tremor then turned into a rumble, and then a clatter, as a large goods tracker came chugging up behind her, pulling a lengthy line of A-framed barrows that were crammed with all kinds of trade items and supplies. She hailed its rider, who then stopped the tracker in a gentle cloud of steam.

"Hau kola," said the rider kindly. "Where are you off to?"

"Kennebec," Kiona replied. "I'm heading to the Samazan Garrison with *very* urgent information."

"Kennebec? Why, that's where we're heading to. Climb aboard, and we'll take you there."

"Why, thank you," she said. "That will mean a lot to me and my tribe in Shenandoah."

Hitching a ride for the remainder of the journey saved her legs after having walked from one end of the island of Gardenia to the other. Kiona heaved a big sigh of relief as she caught sight of one of the many myrestones that dotted the five-mile radius of her destination, Kennebec, a vibrant seaport where people from realms both near and far came to trade within its bustling markets.

She used this as an opportunity to sell her fanglop pelts. And it was here, within the overcrowding, that she accidentally bumped into a cautious man who was carrying an armful of wares: boxes, pelts, and many necessary items spilt everywhere.

"Oh, I'm so sorry," apologised Kiona as she helped him pick up the goods. "Markets here get very busy during the time of Falling Leaves."

"So are the markets in Retania; it's a chore I've grown to accept," replied the man, showing some politeness with a chortle. "Even when this is my first time here in Gardenia."

“What just happened, Isonash?” came a voice suddenly.

“I told you that you were carrying too much! You should have let me carry some!” added another.

Those voices were familiar to Kiona. “Abenanka! Rui-Lin!”

She stood up to greet her old friends as Rui-Lin, for her small size, lifted most of the man’s heavy goods with ease.

“You know her, Abenanka?” the man asked in sudden surprise.

“Kiona and I go way back. We try to meet whenever I travel to Gardenia,” justified Abenanka cheerfully, only for that mood to change like the weather when she noticed Kiona’s sad expression. “Why, Kiona, what’s wrong?”

Kiona heaved a huge sigh as she began her story, trying desperately not to cry.

"Shenandoah was raided by Eresh Kigal two days ago…" Kiona told them sadly. "She massacred the gifted, rounded up all the children, and butchered some of their parents and relations while trying to protect them… I had just returned from the nearby village of Kimiaiya when it happened… I was in time only to see my mother and father slain when trying to protect my little brother."

"Oh, not your father?" Rui-Lin spoke with grief. "I've… Always enjoyed a good arm-wrestle with him."

"She abducted Achak as a keepsake… Her skyark flew south-easterly before it vanished…" continued Kiona, "I travelled all the way to the Samazan Garrison to find help with getting my little brother and the children back… I was wondering if Serena can help me."

"She'll be more than honoured to help a friend," Abenanka responded with a hopeful smile, bravely trying to lift everyone's spirits. "We'll take you to her now, and along the way, I can introduce you to my childhood friend, Isonash."

"Irankarapte, Kiona," he formally introduced. "My apologies for our abrupt introduction."

"Think nothing of it; it was my carelessness..."

Abenanka laughed. "All is forgiven, Kiona."

"Needless to say, that was my first experience in a new country I'll never forget," smiled Isonash.

"Isonash only arrived in Gardenia yesterday and is still getting used to your customs," Abenanka explained to Kiona. "He can be shy at first, but he'll soon warm up like a properly stoked boiler."

"So long as he doesn't blow," snickered Rui-Lin.

"Since when have I ever blown?" Isonash snorted as they made their way out of Kennebec and onto the long causeway that led them towards the Samazan Garrison.

The Discovery

The garrison belonged to The Coalition of Independent Realms, which functioned as the prominent defenders of Gardenia. Although friendly to locals, Kiona can tell when entering through its vast gatehouse and courtyard that the people here are armed and ready for action at any given moment. She instantly felt secure once people who knew her gave her their greetings; then she heard herself called by someone who zipped over to them from the other end of the courtyard like a bolt of lightning.

"Kiona, what a surprise."

"Abigail, what a surprise," retorted Rui-Lin. "I swear, with the speed you're going at, you'd probably be able to run on water."

"Impressed?" she said squarely to Kiona. "I've improved my record since the last time we met."

"You haven't even lost a mile, Abigail," Kiona sighed. "I wish I could say the same for my little brother," she added dolefully.

As soon as she told Abigail about her brother's capture, her friend wasted no time in taking Kiona to see Serena while the others delivered their goods. Serena, who had bright white hair, was in the charter room with another friend called Zoe, mapping out "The Eresh Kigal Incidents" that occurred throughout the region and beyond. The boys, Jabari and Kwahu, were heavily focused on another matter until Kwahu became incredibly surprised at seeing his cousin Kiona at the garrison. Then Kiona told everyone the whole story.

"This is no obvious decoy tactic," Serena concluded. "You're not the first to describe which direction her skyark went after a raid. Zoe and I have since been keeping track." She showed Kiona their charted world map.

"With all the information we have gathered so far, including yours," observed Zoe, "it looks as if Eresh Kigal is making her way to Dagger Teeth Pass on the continent of Cornelia. That's one treacherous mountain range."

"Treacherous enough for a ruthless criminal like her to be hiding in," Kiona suspected, bravely clenching her heart tightly. "I have a strong hunch that is where she has taken my little Achak and the children, and if so, then that's where I'm going."

Of course, upon hearing this, Kwahu hesitated by telling Kiona how dangerous the journey would be. Though after witnessing her determination, willing to risk everything to save her little brother and the children, and since she was supported by the now wary chronicles, Serena and Zoe, he eventually conceded, on condition that he accompanies her on the journey.

Jabari insisted that they should get permission from Saga Saul before heading off: as this was an emergency that permission was readily granted. Since The Coalition were busy combating the Dragoons' invasion of Afallon, it became very difficult to spare some of their troops for the task of finding Eresh Kigal. With established volunteers, Saga Saul recommended that they go on a reconnaissance mission. Kwahu was given a beacon in case they get into trouble or find anything suspicious, so that The Coalition would know where to find them.

Soon the five friends, accompanied by Isonash, Abenanka, and Rui-Lin, who all wanted to come along, embarked on a skyark bound for Belladina, the capital of Tovaro, the principality where Dagger Teeth Pass is located. And once they were flying high above the pass, they boarded a pteron to take them closer to their destination.

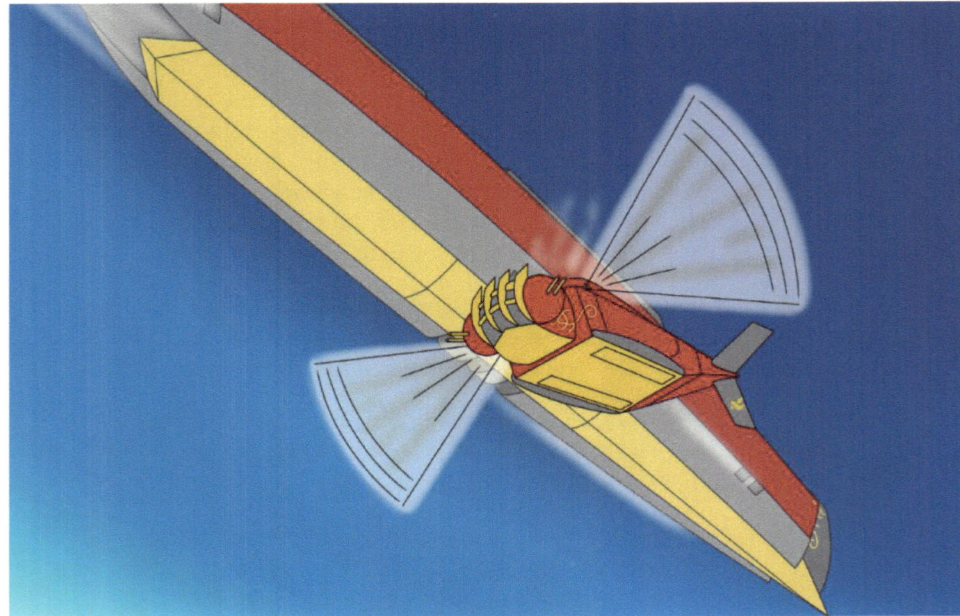

Dagger Teeth Pass is notorious for its extreme blizzards and heavy snowfalls. Not the sort of weather for anyone to be walking or flying in, as they almost crashed-landed onto a cliff edge. It was only thanks to the pteron's riders, Abigail and Zoe and their quick reflexes, that they avoided the danger and touched down safely onto firmer ground.

No sooner were they outside facing the cold than they discovered two pairs of footprints in the snow; they were fresh and still visible through the blizzard that tried fiercely to cover them up. The footprints led them to a ledge that they then began to follow. Knowing how unforgivable the pass is, the friends kept their guard up as the ridge got narrower and narrower.

Suddenly, a section of the ledge gave way, and Kiona fell… Only to be saved by two women on the other side of the gap.

"I've got you," said one, wearing nighteye armour, as they pulled Kiona to safety. "Are you okay?"

"Colder than shaken, but I'm alright," Kiona replied, much relieved.

"We've just made camp. Come with us," the other woman said. The freezing friends followed them towards the glow of a welcoming fire, sheltered from the biting wind within a deep cavern. In the flickering light, the two women revealed themselves, to the relief of the others, as friends they already knew. One, dressed in yellow and red with a navy-blue blindfold, is The Masked Piper. When the other woman took off her helmet, everyone gasped.

"Princess Roso!" exclaimed Abigail. "What are you doing here?"

"The same reason you're all here, I suppose," she enquired. "Since my guards and The Coalition cannot do a job that is extremely significant, I thought that I should do it myself. Fortunately, I met The Masked Piper while travelling up the pass, as she too is hunting Eresh Kigal, who has kidnapped children from my country and many other places. From what people told me of her skyark's direction, I figured that Dagger Teeth Pass is where she could have taken them."

"That's what I thought when Serena and Zoe showed me their reports," Kiona told her.

"You as well? What a remarkable coincidence," the Princess spoke with surprise, and a friendly conversation began. From then on, as she had helped to save Kiona's life, the two became best friends.

"Is it just me, or is it getting hot in here?"

"Oh, really, Isonash, of all people."

"No, Rui-Lin, I feel hot too," The Masked Piper corrected. "And I don't think our fire has anything to do with it."

"Did you explore the cavern thoroughly when you first got here?" Zoe questioned.

"We had not long since arrived to take shelter when we heard you coming," countered The Masked Piper.

"You won't believe this!" Abigail's voice echoed from the far end of the cavern.

It took them a while to catch up to her, but once they did, they were greeted by a strong smell of sulphur and the gurgling ruptures of an enormous lava pool. Abigail pointed them towards the familiar shape of Eresh Kigal's skyark, landed beside the hidden fortress of an underground lair. Kiona and Princess Roso's suspicions could not have been more accurate, for they had finally found where Eresh Kigal had taken the children.

The Rescue

Kwahu placed the beacon in a hidden crevice as they crept stealthily down into the lair. By sneaking through and taking out a couple of unsuspecting smugglers, they arrived at a heavy door that presumably led down to the cells.

Just moments away from turning the handle, a fierce slam, followed by disgruntled muttering and approaching footsteps, back-peddled them into hiding positions, so that when this angry smuggler came bursting through the door like a fierce tempest, they were able to see to it that his enraged fire was immediately fizzled out.

Retracing the smuggler's steps by entering through the door, descending the stairs, and opening the door to the cells, the friends took down many more smugglers who had been horribly treating the children as less than animals. Realising what was happening and recognising who the friends served when their cell doors were broken open, the children's misery turned into rapture for their heroes.

Kiona, meanwhile, was more anxious than ever to find her little brother, and relief came when she noticed the children from her tribe. They pointed her to a cell at the far end of the chamber where she found him, frail and frightened, in a corner. He had cried so much that his eyes were sealed shut. He was reduced to wearing his torn underwear and headdress, had terrible cuts and bruises all over his body, and, on closer examination, it looked as if all his fingers were missing from his right hand. Abigail was already there, comforting and attending to his wounds.

"It must have been really scary for you," Abigail sympathised, as Kiona calmly approached him.

"It's alright, Achak. I'm here now," Kiona said as Abigail gave him to her. She gently pressed his head to her chest, which relaxed him as soon as his ears encountered her calm and soothing heartbeat.

"K…Ki…o…na…" he spoke feebly while his sister hushed him.

"Try not to speak, Achak. You need to rest."

"These are such ruthless cuts," The Masked Piper said while gently feeling his hand.

"I noticed that when I found him," informed Abigail, "He was terrified of me when I got close. He has never been afraid of *me* before?"

"How could people do such cold-hearted things?" sighed Princess Roso, who couldn't stand to witness such suffering done to innocent children.

"Might I suggest you allow him to stay with me?" recommended The Masked Piper to Kiona. "He'll be safe from Eresh Kigal with the gifted I'm protecting."

Kiona knew that her heartbeat is the only thing that helps her little brother to sleep… She cannot bear to leave him after coming all this way to rescue him… Nevertheless, she gave her brother to The Masked Piper and Princess Roso while she and Abigail set off to free the rest of the children. Isonash and Kwahu then arrived in the cell. Kwahu was enraged at the sight of Achak's right hand, while Isonash, the Princess, and The Masked Piper, although never having seen Achak before, could not help but sense that they had already somehow met.

Soon, the friends began to escort the entrapped children out of their cells, with The Masked Piper carrying Achak. They knew it would not take long for the smugglers within the lair itself to discover that they had intruders, and sure enough, they were waiting for them. This quickly became a stalemate; the situation reduced to one small gap of opportunity for the friends and the children to escape, and only Kiona knew how to accomplish it.

She stood forward calmly, full of faith and spirit, determined to give her own life in exchange for the safety of her friends and the children. Achak was horrified and desperately tried to clamber out of The Masked Piper's arms, reaching blindly for his sister when he realised what she was about to do.

Then it happened…

Kiona was struck violently in the heart… Not by the shot from one of the smugglers, but from the shock of where this shot hit… As if time stood still, through her trembling eyes, she saw her little brother fling himself from the startled Masked Piper's arms before falling, like a lone forest leaf, abruptly landing with a violent thump on the ground in front of the stunned Princess, the intended target.

Another shot was fired… killing one of the smugglers who carelessly got in the way of the Princess. Those two shots were conducted by none other than Eresh Kigal herself. Her presence was enough to make the children tremble with fear. Not even the heat from the lava outside can compete against this icy cold atmosphere as she gazed mutely towards the friends.

The smugglers were also terrified the moment she entered the frame. They knew full well that no one should ever mess with her, as some of the children's relatives and parents, like Kiona's, had done while trying to defend them.

Eresh Kigal coldly looked down at Achak for a moment. Then she glared at his sister. Kiona stood her ground, for it became apparent that Achak's sacrifice had inevitably caused a rift, a fulfilment of something that dislodged Eresh Kigal's patience once she discovered her unintentional faux pas.

Princess Roso collected Achak as they made a hasty retreat back towards the cells. With her strength, Rui-Lin smashed the door lock shut behind them, preventing Eresh Kigal from following and, hopefully, holding her off until The Coalition arrive.

Princess Roso kissed and thanked Achak for saving her life as she lay him on a bed of straw in one of the cells. Abenanka and Zoe then tried to tend the wound on his chest, but it was clear that the damage was too great. He became paler and paler from the massive blood loss, and as a result, his breathing became shallower. Anxious children gathered round.

"It looks like you'll be seeing our parents before me, Achak," Kiona spoke gently, trying to lighten this dark scene as she lay with him, resting his head comfortably on her chest while covering his wound with a cloth... Then, privately, she spoke to him encouragingly...

"It is no big secret that from the day you were born, I've always wished for there to be a way to conceal you within my heart as a means of protecting you. Now's the opportunity for us to ultimately fulfil that wish. We can be whole again, just like we were before our conceptions, after The Father separated us for this fulfilling destiny.

"I will never forget what you have done for the Princess of Tovaro, and the people of Afallon, with lifting 'Emrys' Curse' through the loss of your fingers, whoever it was that did this to you... You are a true hero."

"I…it… is… done…"

Those were the only words he managed to say as his life finally faded. To everyone's amazement, his body slowly transformed itself into a gentle glow so small that it can fit into the palm of Kiona's hand.

She then pressed the tiny light deeply into her heart. She felt his presence entering within her, his warmth and comfort circulating all around her body, drying away her tears and increasing her joy a hundredfold.

"It is done," she responded happily as the two became one, with nothing now physically left of him except for his blood-stained bandages, his torn underwear, and his headdress.

No one can explain what had happened, not even the children, for some were sobbing that another child had succumbed to Eresh Kigal's vicious cruelty.

Naturally, to comfort her after her loss, The Masked Piper went to hug Kiona. Yet no sooner did she press her chest against Kiona's than a sharp pain struck her in her eyes. Blood began to flow out from behind the blindfold for a moment before they were cleansed by the fresh, sweet saltiness of her tears. To conceal her identity, Isonash and Abenanka took her into one of the cells so that they could tend to her in secret. They gave her a damp cloth to wipe away the blood and tears, but just as she was drying them, her eyes showed signs of blinking, which led her to open them for the first time in years.

"Tures, your eyes!" exclaimed Isonash.

"Hasinaw, what happened?" asked Abenanka.

"It is done. After eight years, he has not forgotten his promise," responded The Masked Piper with a smile.

Kiona's Heart

It was a long time before the door began to give way, and the friends braced themselves, only to be greeted warmly by The Coalition in their stone-powered battle armour. They were accompanied by Chronicle Sorcha, the bold and strong right hand to Saga Saul. Kiona had already acquainted herself with Sorcha, who is also a firm friend to both Serena and Zoe. Sorcha and many of The Coalition were over the moon to see them and the children safe and sound.

"Aye, that uggin itch is gaen fur noo," she shortly remarked.

It was from Sorcha that the friends learned, while they were escorting the children to the skyarks that would take them home, that Eresh Kigal was long gone when they arrived. All the smugglers in the lair were already massacred: no doubt from Eresh Kigal's exasperation that the friends thankfully avoided.

It was evening when Kiona and Kwahu returned by pteron to Shenandoah, an enchanting town on the west coast of Gardenia, made up of homes built within ancient giant trees that towered over the landscape.

Once their pteron landed, the children were overjoyed to be reunited with their surviving parents and relations again; charitable families happily adopted those who were less fortunate. As Kwahu went to talk to his father, the chief of the town, Kiona set off home, where she knew her grandmother would be waiting. She was unexpectedly calm after Kiona told her what had happened. She knew that her granddaughter is safe, and her grandson's presence now resides within his sister's heart.

Kiona can feel his presence, even while she was soaking in the bathing pool with its calming waterfall gushing over her tired shoulders.

"It's like how we used to bathe together when you were Achak," she thought while relaxing in the gentle laps and flows of the water. "It's comforting to know that we can now experience this together as one."

With her heart glowing as though to outshine the stone-powered lamps, Kiona happily closed her eyes as Achak's fond memories started to flow into her. Yet she didn't want to think about the awful things he experienced in Eresh Kigal's captivity: *they* are reserved for future evidence.

When Kiona was retiring to bed, she decided to sleep in Achak's room. She made herself comfortable under the eyetler hide, snuggling into the soft fur that still had his scent, recollecting the contentment she felt when resting her brother's head on her chest; listening to her heartbeat that would always have him out like a light. She thought deeply about her brother.

"You probably wish to see me too," she thought as she went happily to sleep.

When she next opened her eyes, she found herself within a room of bright, comforting light, adorned with many beautiful things made from transparent gold and precious stones. Unsurprised, she knew that all these things were familiar to her. She was then compelled to head towards a special doorway that led to the heart of this pure mansion of hers.

She saw her little brother waiting for her in the distance as she entered
the doorway. His right-hand fingers were sown back on by unseen hands,
indicated by the white lines to where they were severed. He appeared to be in his
thirties, yet small for his age, half the size of her, and easy to mistake for a child.
Even she looked ten years older, and they were both wearing pure white robes.
Kiona ran over, and the two siblings embraced each other like reunited long-lost
family members.

"Oh, Levtiqvah," chirped Kiona. "I knew since the day you were born
as my little brother that we were together again. Your incarnation and love for
my heartbeat are too analogous to miss."

"I'm just happy to be back within your heart again, Tiqvah," smiled her
brother as he nestled within her loving arms. "And a good thing too, as The
Father's Presence would like to speak to you. Although you cannot see him for
now, he has always been within you since your incarnation as Kiona, just as he's
within me since my incarnation as Achak."

Hearing a voice from all directions, The Presence spoke to Kiona soothingly and with utmost importance.

Kiona, from the start, is an incarnated feminine angel called Tiqvah, who represents hope. In contrast, her little brother, Achak, is her unique masculine heart-angel called Levtiqvah, who represents the hearts of women that he can read, listen to, and understand. Both are symbiotic and were created to work together. Achak's death and the reunion with his sister's heart was the signal she'd been waiting for, as it marked the beginning of a crucial path The Father planned for them since the dawn of time.

"No matter what happens now, we will never be apart," assured Levtiqvah.

"As we were. As we shall be," agreed Kiona.

She then remembered that her heart tends to shrink whenever he is grieved. However, in this case, as she knew he would, he was shrinking in comfort to his sister. As her heart, this gave Kiona the notion to joyfully tuck him deep within her chest.

"There you go, Levtiqvah. Back where you belong," she smiled.

This is not embarrassing to Levtiqvah, nor is he aroused by this, for to be within her chest is to him the equivalent of being within the most comfortable bed in the world, and it didn't take long for him to settle down as his sister's heartbeat, despite the fact that angels do not sleep. The soft walls of any woman's chest helps to amplify the heartbeat around him, making it easy for Levtiqvah to understand them with pinpoint accuracy. In return, the women are rewarded with the warmth and comfort that delights them, as he's doing for Kiona, especially now that the two are reunited as one.

And *that* experience is only a sample of what Levtiqvah can provide for Kiona and all women.

Kiona woke up the following morning, fully refreshed and filled with such incredible joy from Levtiqvah. When she told her grandmother about her dream as she was eating breakfast, it made her grandmother remember meeting one of Tiqvah's brothers before Kiona and Achak were born, who told her that The Father had a unique purpose for Tiqvah and Levtiqvah that they would have to face together.

"When I was a little girl, I heard stories about the appearance of a woman called The Maid of the Heart with a heart full of hope," her grandmother revealed. "I never would have imagined her to be my own granddaughter."

"The Father works with those who have a lot of faith in him, as you do. Your bloodline was chosen for that reason," smiled Kiona. "I vowed to use my gifts responsibly for The Father's Son."

"I know you will," beamed her grandmother with confident wisdom. "Your cheerful nature, with a combination of hope, is just what this troubled world needs."

The Forest Trial

A few days had passed since Kiona's return from Dagger Teeth Pass. After attending her parents' funeral, Chief Samoset handed the torch of Forest Ringmaster to her. She would have been her father's successor anyway, as Achak, who was seven and born gifted, lacked the vital components needed to become a Ringmaster. She is also a very keen gardener, which made her more than qualified to be a part of the Trials of Maturity, a traditional custom to the people of Gardenia. There are four Ringmasters in each Trial, one for each season, and they are located within the four major towns across the country: Shenandoah being one of them. Each Trial is designed to help participants understand the seasons, learn to grow and hunt food for survival, and cope with the constant changes throughout the years as they mature in life.

The Forest Trial is to teach the virtues of harvest in the time of Falling Leaves, to reap their own rewards from the golden days of the High Sun. The responsibility thrilled her as she quickly adjusted to her new role. With years of skilled training from her father, she waited with eager anticipation for her first participant.

One day, Isonash arrived to check on Kiona, as well as to introduce her to his twin sister, Hasinaw. The two looked so similar that, if it were not for their voices and their robes called attushes, she would think she was seeing double. Within the empty stadium, they mentioned in secret that Hasinaw is, of course, The Masked Piper. And with her intention to protect and look after the persecuted gifted, Kiona promised to keep it so.

"So that's what Levtiqvah meant when he asked me to be patient for eight years," Hasinaw said once Kiona revealed who she and her brother are.

"He's certainly one of The Father's angels that truly keeps his word," added Isonash. "He was like a part of our family when we first met him back in Retania. He usually takes the form of a little boy and would appear mainly to my sister here. Stands to reason since his gift is to understand the hearts of women and not that of men... Probably for the best."

Kiona then changed the subject. "So, Hasinaw, you said you competed in Gardenia's Trials of Maturity?"

"Twelve years ago, after acquiring the Wold Talisman, I was struck blind by the eyes of an aracktor," she explained. "Since then, I've been unable to continue," and she showed Kiona the two Talismans she had earned so far.

"With The Father's Son accompanying Levtiqvah within your heart, restoring my sight the moment I hugged you last time we met and, already learnt from our friends that you have succeeded to your father's role as Forest Ringmaster," Hasinaw told Kiona, "I decided that now is the perfect time for me to finally complete the Trials of Maturity. Even though I've been training for years to recompete without my sight."

"I'm already considering competing in the Trials myself," admitted Isonash. "It will probably give me the edge I've been lacking."

"I look forward to giving you the Forest Trial next year, Isonash," encouraged Kiona. "You can start learning from your sister while I evaluate her skills."

Each of the Trials' three tests took place within specially constructed areas within each stadium. For instance, with the Forest Trial, the first test is to sweep the leaves evenly within the stadium's arena. The second test involves gathering the select harvest from the stadium's field. And the third test is to transport the gathered harvest up the stadium's tree, the tallest in the town and where Kiona's home is located, and deposit them within a storeroom above.

On her third test, Hasinaw slipped several times on the wet bark and leaves caused by torrential rain the night before, but she was undeterred and determined not to give up too easily. As she steadily climbed, she sang and danced with high spirits. Isonash was singing and dancing along, too. This is part of their culture from Retania, and Hasinaw was still singing and dancing after she got to the treetops and deposited the goods.

Finally, as with all four Trials, came the test of mind, stealth, and agility in the form of a game called Clutch. This game is the ultimate challenge between the participant and the Ringmaster: both wielding Clutch Staffs, long poles with pelted mitts attached to the ends. The aim is to use their clutch staff to catch the ball and fling it at their five goals at each end of the stadium's arena. The first one to make an All-Four by hitting their central goal last wins.

Isonash watched with interest as the two girls competed against each other in the game, both fixated on the ball, ensuring it did not touch the ground, their already hit goal, and their central goal early for fear of starting all over. At first, Kiona had the upper hand from years of training with her father. Thinking she had victory in her sights, she then got distracted, wondering what Hasinaw would do when she lost and what her strategy would be to win when she next tries again. Kiona was so sidetracked that she allowed an opening to be exposed, and Hasinaw saw her chance. With one mighty jump and hurl, she triumphed over Kiona and successfully gained her All-Four… All with her eyes closed.

"Still have it in me," she remarked, and even her brother had to agree, principally as they knew each other inside out.

At last, Kiona presented Hasinaw with her Forest Talisman to signify her accomplishment.

"Only one more to go now," chuckled Kiona. "It looks like there are still some things I haven't learned from my father; you've helped me to realise that. It was so much fun. As the new Forest Ringmaster, it was such a delight to have you as my first participant."

"Anything for a friend: the proprietor to our old friend," said Hasinaw as she gave Kiona a warming hug. As their chests pressed together, Kiona noticed the biggest smile on Hasinaw's face and tears, like a babbling brook, gently flowing from her restored eyes.

Kiona and Isonash cannot see it, but Kiona can sense, from within her heart, that her brother had jumped in to visit Hasinaw's. What seemed to be a moment to Kiona is an eternity to Levtiqvah, and she felt that the conversation he and Hasinaw's inner conscience were having was very much indeed a long one.

The Retanian Twins
Thursday, 30th September 332 (1734)

The Snow Angel

The twins, Isonash and Hasinaw, are from Retania, a group of islands that are extremely far away from Gardenia: almost on the opposite side of the northern part of the world. Abenanka, a good friend of both the twins and Kiona, is also from Retania, which, along with Gardenia, its island neighbour off the south-west coast called Afallon, Luso in the south, as well as a few more members, are all part of what is known as the Mawchick Alliance.

The Retanians were once the Ainus; the Lusoans were the Portuguese; and the Afallons were the Cymrus before a devastating event took place three hundred and thirty-two years ago, on the 2nd of July 1402, called "The Firestorm", which their ancestors survived, either within caves or awoke from comas centuries later. Serena and Sorcha are prime examples of the latter and, as such, were now referred to as relics.

The year is 332 A.T. (After "The Firestorm"), or, to a relic, 1734.

One fine blustery morning, Kiona cheerfully strolled past a myrestone that pointed her towards the sun-shone Kennebec and Samazan Garrison. She was not in a rush, just taking her time as she had started her trek early, days before she was scheduled to meet up with the twins, along with Abenanka and Rui-Lin, before travelling together to Retania.

She had been there once with her father when she was very young, and it was from there that she met and befriended Abenanka. For this reason, she thought it would be nice to revisit the islands.

Of course, their mode of travel was by skyark from the garrison, which also functioned as a point of departure for those wishing to journey to faraway places: just so long as that place had the protection of The Coalition.

While waiting for their skyark to arrive, they were approached by Chronicle Sorcha and Saga Saul, who thanked Kiona for helping them rescue the children from last week. They respectfully commiserate at the loss of her little brother when he saved Princess Roso's life.

"Why show sorrow for a journey that has already begun?" she happily reassured them. "You know as well as I, through faith, of where he and my parents have gone."

"I'm just checking how you're coping," responded Saga Saul. "I am glad to see that you've overcome your loss so quickly. Envious from those who had lost loved ones to not just Eresh Kigal, but also to when the Dragoons successfully conquered The Emeralds: trouncing our finest soldiers with one fell swoop."

A curious thought overwhelmed him as he spoke. "I thought for certain the Afallons would suffer a similar fate. It was only after you left for Dagger Teeth Pass that things started turning more in their favour when, after a huge coastal invasion, and against all odds, the Afallons managed to push the Yin-Lung Dynasty back into the sea."

"My uncle, Chief Samoset, rejected another protection offer from those Dragoons five days ago," Kiona verified. "And that General Tang-Lang, as she walked out, acted more indignant than the last time."

"Sounds like she'll be bringing more of a military, rather than just a simple escort, on her next visit," reckoned Isonash.

"That's what I was thinking," Saga Saul mused before giving an order to Chronicle Sorcha. "Pass a message to the Deena Garrison and its renovations. See to it that Shenandoah and the west coast of Gardenia are provided with extra protection from any possible attacks."

"Aye, Saga," she responded before departing.

"Once again, to all, thank you," he said as he left in the opposite direction.

Once in the air, heading north-north-easterly towards Retania through the Starry Heavens above, sitting comfortably in the lounge with its light refracted walls, an alternative replacement to windows in their world as a means of protection against curse storms, the friends began discussing about the Afallons and their surprising victory against a creeping enemy that threatened theirs, and the friend's whole way of life.

"Every day, another expanse of land is seized," Isonash sighed.

"The Innocent massacred, their belongings taken, and whole communities destroyed through false promises of utopia and equality," shuddered Rui-Lin delicately. "It's a miracle that my family and I managed to escape their oppressive regime."

"I'm just relieved to hear that our troubled ally has found the spirit to fight back," Kiona heaved, "and it couldn't have come at a better time."

"So am I," agreed Abenanka. "But let's leave that subject for the time being. Do you have anything else you would like to share or discuss?"

"How generous of you to ask, Abenanka," Kiona replied. "Because I happen to have something I've been meaning to ask the twins…"

"If it's to do with how we met Levtiqvah, then I am more than happy to explain," Hasinaw interrupted cheerfully as she began.

"My brother had already mentioned to you in the Forest Trial Stadium that Levtiqvah usually takes the form of a little boy. Before coming to The Father's Son, we did not refer to him as an angel, but a kamuy, a spiritual being that, in our culture, was not too difficult to miss when I first met him many years ago, on one cold, snowy night.

"I was returning after a long trek, gathering firewood from the forest and collecting essentials from the nearest town. Even so, they were both a considerable distance from our home, called a cise. Isonash was recovering from a broken leg, and our parents had the flu, so I was tasked with supplying them with the vital things they needed. On my way back, a blizzard began to build, and… With my pockets and bags so packed full of necessary items… I cannot spare one: not a crumb.

"I had just got over most of the problematic parts of the journey when I caught sight of something curled up in the snow. Thinking it was a fanglop, I kept my distance. Yet curiosity got the better of me when I noticed that the shape was not moving. As I got closer, I was astounded to discover that it was not a fanglop, but a tiny boy in white robes, trembling in the snow.

"He was unbelievably small, about the size of a mouse, and had all the looks of forlornness weighing down on him, as though he had lost something… Or someone… Having no spare room amongst my supplies and needing my hands free to get through the shocking weather… This all left me with a difficult decision, but I couldn't leave him alone to freeze… It makes me glad to be a woman when I decided to conceal him within my chest when it would have been naturally impossible for a man to do… A touch unorthodox, I'll agree… At least in there, he would be warm and safe.

"After I had walked a mile, his presence gradually became like a properly stoked fire. He warmed my heart so much that the biting wind and the freezing cold snow no longer bothered me, and, before I knew it, I was greeted by the actual stoked fire of home.

"After delivering the goods, I still kept him within my chest as I went to sleep in my own bed: he was comfortable in there anyway… But when I woke up the next morning, he was no longer there. Instead, he was now in his normal child-size, staring out of the opened kamuy puyar, a doorway for the gods in our culture. I suspected that he had been waiting for me, as he turned round with a friendly smile and said, "Thank you for rekindling my hopes," before disappearing with a sunbeam. That was not the last I saw of him," Hasinaw concluded, "as, since then, Levtiqvah would appear to me on many occasions."

"I got the chance to see him when we were trapped inside that avalanche," reminded Abenanka. "He was the one who got us out of it."

"Honestly, I thought you two were suffering from snow-stroke," Isonash admitted. "That was until we played our favourite prank on our parents by exchanging our attushes. I thought it backfired on me when my old girlfriend, Hurenitay, appeared and mistook Hasinaw for me when finally expressing her love. It was only when I came to believe in Levtiqvah's existence while confessing who I am to her that he ultimately revealed himself.

"Thankfully, he wasn't the real Hurenitay. Although he did play her part very well," he added lastly.

Kiona laughed as Levtiqvah's memories flowed into her, making it seem like *she'd* encountered them all those years ago. Understanding him, she proceeded to hug her friends so that Levtiqvah could make his presence known once more.

"Definitely not atlanmy, thank goodness," sighed Rui-Lin.

"Of course it isn't," Isonash huffed. "Levtiqvah would still have to be alive as Achak for that to be possible. When in the form of Hurenitay, he and Hasinaw…" then muttering to himself. "…*And no doubt Hurenitay, it has her name written all over it*…" before concluding. "…They at least planned it all to get my attention that he was there."

"Even so, I do find him very handsome," admitted Rui-Lin as she rested her head snugly on Kiona's chest, blushing with much affection. "Never thought your little brother would grow up to become the right size for little old me."

"Women and angels don't mix, Rui-Lin," Hasinaw addressed, but that didn't stop her from dreaming.

A Day Out

It was dark when they arrived at the Kimuyay Garrison, and as expected in Retania at this time of year, it was very cold indeed with the early snowfalls. Kiona was well prepared, having brought her warmest under-pelt, which she put on the following morning after spending the night in a cise they'd rented.

Gentle snowflakes raced and danced throughout the crisp, cool air while her breath, which now formed into clouds of vapour outdoors, signalled a sharp awakening from the warm stupor of indoors.

"It's my turn now, Levtiqvah," Kiona thought happily as she stretched her arms wide and her chest high. "Knowing you're safe within my heart again, I'm sure you can keep *me* warm while staying with my friends in Retania, just like you did for Hasinaw when she helped you."

As with every morning upon waking, after a quick breakfast and when that typical intuition comes calling, Kiona set off to fulfil that task, only to find herself in a queue outside a thatched structure called a menokoru. Hasinaw was also waiting, as was Rui-Lin in her under-pelt, who entered when Abenanka emerged.

There is a small hut next to it that looked smarter and more mature than the menokoru, and it was at that moment that Isonash came walking out of it.

"Oh, thank you, Isonash," sighed Kiona, "I'm so desperate right now."

Isonash calmly barred her from entering. "This is an asinru, Kiona," he informed her sorrowfully and embarrassingly. "In our culture, this is for men only. Menokoru is for the women."

"Oh, my mistake, Isonash." Kiona apologised. "I'm more used to the indoor-unisex-lavatories in Gardenia than queuing for ages in the snow. At least you're someone, I can tell, who's very honest and understanding to us women."

"He is," justified Abenanka. "He doesn't think it's fair for men to have better things than women, even when this is cultural to our people in Retania… Personally, I don't mind it."

"Discussing the privies again? I thought we'd got over that by now!" Rui-Lin snorted as she emerged from the menokoru, and Hasinaw entered. "Why don't we discuss something else, like, how does it feel to have an angel for a heart residing within you, Kiona? I bet he's all warm and comfortable in there."

"It's more than just a feeling, Rui-Lin. It is a fact that he's always with me," Kiona hinted when placing her hand over her heart. Then she began romanticising distant memories. "Oh, I can just remember the day my mother gave birth to him… how I was ready to receive him… cut his umbilical cord and…"

There was a long silence from her startled friends.

"Oh dear! I got carried away with the details, didn't I?" Kiona asked when noticing their still expressions. Realising that she had spoken too openly, notably when they nodded in response, she embarrassingly entered the menokoru as Hasinaw, at that moment, reappeared.

It was some time before Kiona emerged from the menokoru. She couldn't stay in it all day! There is much to see on this unique island that has just started its time of Cold Nights. Isonash, Hasinaw, and Rui-Lin had been up at the crack of dawn fishing for salmon for that evening's dinner. With the task secured and their catch safely in the storage shed called a pu, the friends decided to travel along the south coast to enjoy some fantastic views.

"Be careful," warned Hasinaw, "the fanglops will be in their white coats now. They're swift enough to bring down the strongest person if the whole warren is alerted."

"The eyetlers are in their coats, too," Kiona observed. "They blend in so well with the lightning trees and snow that you cannot make them out, apart from their eyes in the antlers."

"Have you ever wondered if the skin covering their face is where their eyes originally were?" Abenanka pondered. "It's amazing to think that when an eyetler is born, it has no antlers and is born blind: yet in a few days, there they are."

A sharp, panpipe-like shrill sound echoed within the trees, followed swiftly by two more that made Kiona stop in her tracks, mesmerised.

"A rare wood s'hesta?" she recognised and said so aloud.

"Correct," responded Hasinaw. "Like Gardenia, Luso, and Afallon, Retania too has its fair share of common and rare wood s'hestas. Yet, unlike them, while you Gardenians have the elusive aaab, our country is home to the Retanian river s'hestas."

"If only you'd been with us when we were fishing, we caught sight of one hunting for salmon nearby," Isonash recounted. "It had to chase off some nasty common wood s'hestas when they tried to steal its catch."

"Wish I could have seen it," sighed Kiona. "With so many common wood s'hestas in Gardenia, it makes it hard to spot my favourite smaller rare wood s'hestas."

"Perhaps tomorrow at dawn, with any luck," Rui-Lin encouraged. "So long as you don't oversleep."

The friends were now wandering along the beach, comprising a compact mixture of snow and sand, when Hasinaw hesitated. In the distance was a large dark shape that resembled a giant spider, motionless and presumably dead, as three common wood s'hestas were pecking at its body, smartly using their noses rather than their eyes, which they had purposely closed.

"Keep your eyes shut," she cautioned. Everyone did so as she continued, "Even when it's dead, an aracktor's eyes can still blind you. I learned the hard way, and I'm not making that mistake again."

With only their ears as their witness, they heard the three s'hestas being abruptly startled and ran off. Next, a huge splash and a thump erupted on the beach, accompanied by powerful flippers and strong jaws snapping and grabbing something before flipping back into the sea. When they opened their eyes to the restored silence, the aracktor's body had disappeared.

"Oh my… I *trust* that wasn't a poi?" Rui-Lin asked concerningly, and, having similar assumptions, the five friends made a hasty retreat off the beach and into the safety of the forest.

The Kitayto of Akari

Rising steam and a sudden temperature change indicated that they were approaching two hot springs. Four of the friends had always known about this tranquil place, and it was indeed a real treat after their long walk on a cold, snowy morning. Isonash had the most minor, banished by the rocks from the giant spring that held the girls' ancient tradition of cheerful conversations.

"While we were on the beach," Kiona told her friends, "I noticed some black peaks that stuck out menacingly on the white horizon."

"That's the kitayto that surrounds the islands of Akari," answered Hasinaw.

"Akari?" Kiona asks them.

"Descendants of the Sisams, the Akaris were our ancient enemies, hell-bent on conquering our islands long ago," described Abenanka. "We don't mention them very often, as it's a difficult and emotional subject to talk about." She abruptly sighed. "Though I might as well explain it to you now."

Abenanka continued, "The Sisams, with their samurai armies, would have succeeded in conquering us Ainus, if it weren't for 'The Firestorm' that made our ancestors go from strength to strength as Retanians. Decades after that event, the predecessors of The Coalition, The Shepherds, arrived at our shores from the west in their flying wooden cloudarks, curiously wanting to learn about our culture, and to help us get back on our feet after 'The Firestorm'.

"They were patient enough so we can learn from them, and we Retanians got along very well. But not the Sisams, renamed the Akaris after the Akari shogunate, who saw The Shepherds as a threat to their traditional ways. So much so that they began harshly taxing any of their people who accepted The Shepherds' beliefs, which eventually boiled over into a rebellion that the shogun's samurais swiftly put down. After that, The Shepherds were expelled from Akari when the shogunate issued the 'sakoku policy'. This law is to ban all foreigners from setting foot on their lands under the penalty of death.

"Unwanted in Akari, The Shepherds were more than welcome in Retania: until the shogun's samurais landed not long after and destroyed almost all of The Shepherd's presence on our islands; by orders of 'sakoku'. That intrusion inflamed us and, with The Shepherd's support, who wasn't willing to abandon us that easily, led to a war of independence against the Akaris. Yet despite the victorious outcome, we knew that they would stop at nothing to expand as far as the eye can see. What we see as Retania… To them, is only Akari.

"It was around that time that The Shepherds were experimenting with their strange stones that were generated from 'The Firestorm': the same stones that we use today. They found that, with them, they were able to form mountains out of water. After a long and complicated discussion, and with the survival of the Retanian way of life crucial, we had no choice but to sever trade from Akari in favour of other nations. Meanwhile, The Shepherds began creating these mountains, the kitayto as we call them, all around the islands of Akari.

"Because of this, the Akaris can no longer trade with anyone. Nor would they be able to go over or under the kitayto, in nor out. The Shepherds made it clear to Akari that, since they'd hypocritically chosen to isolate themselves from the world, then the world would isolate itself from them! This may seem harsh, but as old oppressors, we believe that they deserved it," Abenanka finished firmly.

"So the Akaris have been imprisoned in there ever since?" Kiona inquired.

"Not for much longer," notified Rui-Lin. "I've heard a rumour that The Aquilas are planning to fly their legionnaires onto those islands."

"They'd never dare!" Abenanka responded harshly. "That would be breaking 'The Doomsday Compact', which clearly states that Akari is to be left alone; no exceptions, no trade, no contact."

"Try telling them that, when they marched their legionnaires into the Iztax Empire, this High Sun passed." Reminded Rui-Lin.

"They've *actually* captured The Capital of the Sun? Talk about poetic justice." Kiona said. "My father told me that when I was very little, the Iztax Empire attempted to annexe The Northern Isles by means of a trading union, including Afallon, Gardenia, The Emeralds, Katalef, and Urcaledon, which is united with Celeste as part of the Ur Alliance. The way they tried to accomplish it was very sneaky, and it was only after we discovered their true intentions, followed by a unanimous vote against them, that their mask finally came off.

"Desperate for our resources, they tried to take our islands by force. But after the combined efforts of our alliance, aided by The Shepherds, and our old enemies, the Ur Alliance and, to a lesser extent, The Emeralds, a bane to Gardenia's existence. We together drove the Iztax Empire from our shores in our own war of independence.

"My father and uncle helped lead the charge with Gwendolyn in the decisive Battle of Gelert in Afallon."

"Yes, I don't think The Aquilas will be using *that* tactic on Akari," Rui-Lin reassured. "As a military might that enjoys showing off its strength, it sees no difficulty going up against a formidable target like the now-dissolved Iztax Empire. With the kitayto surrounding Akari, and with The Aquila's air superiority, I'm telling you now! It'll be just like a ravenous s'hesta in a chicken coop."

"I can see where you're coming from," agreed Hasinaw gravely.

"The Aquilas would say… '*It's for protection against The Dragoon Menace.*'… *I'd* see it as an excuse for a land-grab," Rui-Lin spoke sarcastically. "Now that The Shepherds are gone, who is to say that they're going to pay attention to outdated pieces of paper? Let's face it! Akari is the perfect strategic location for getting close to the Dragoon's capital."

"That would explain why the Yin-Lung Dynasty were so desperate to get Gardenia on their side to counter the Northern Roman Empire's capital," pondered Kiona as everything seemed to add up. "Perhaps there *is* some truth to this."

"It doesn't seem all that long ago that The Shepherds tore themselves apart with their Civil War," Abenanka sighed a little while later as they continued their walk.

"We've always got to find hope, Abenanka," comforted Kiona, and for the rest of that frigid day, the five friends tried their best not to think about the Yin-Lung Dynasty and the Northern Roman Empire, as it wouldn't do either their digestion or their sightseeing any good.

They made sure to stay well clear of broad rivers, as a poi fish can easily drag itself into shallow water as they do on beaches, just as one presumably did when gulping down the dead aracktor. Pois are so notoriously conniving that they're even known to bump people off boats to swallow them whole. People, sorry to say, are one of their primary prey.

Kiona and Isonash

The next day, Kiona woke up very early to join her friends on their fishing trip. She managed to catch sight of not one, but two Retanian river s'hestas, with a nighteye swooping by, and a rare wood s'hesta as a bonus that ate whatever was left of the river s'hesta's catch. Her heart raced with joy from the sight of her favourite animal, which gazed up at her and presented itself by spreading its wings. Her joy was magnified by Levtiqvah's response, who was experiencing her excitement simultaneously.

Isonash quietly gave Kiona a piece of salmon meat to see if she could get it to come closer. The bird put its cautiousness aside, and Kiona was able to stroke the shell on its back while feeding it. It didn't scamper off in a hurry when it decided to return to the forest.

"Now, who does that s'hesta remind you of?" hinted Rui-Lin to Isonash, chortling.

"It's not every day you see a wild animal eagerly wanting to be petted," Hasinaw speculated to Kiona, "not even for the salmon meat you gave it."

Kiona had wanted to do something exciting with her friends. She also wanted to know more about Isonash, so when he, with Abenanka, decided to visit their childhood town, Kiona was more than delighted to come along. Hasinaw and Rui-Lin had to finish a few things back in the cise but did say they'd meet up with them once their tasks were completed.

The town, called Hureatni, not far from the Kimuyay Garrison, is a bustling place that sells many fine goods, from attushes and wood carvings to charcoal-cooked mahiz and salmon. Both Abenanka and Kiona fondly remembered their childhood here, where they met and became best friends. As if their bond had now been strengthened, Abenanka told Kiona how she generously took Levtiqvah in, treating him like her own son after saving her and Hasinaw from an avalanche. This was all done from her caring heart after she noticed how forlorn he looked.

Abenanka was just about to explain the part when Levtiqvah had to leave her for eight years, when a group of over-excited people quickly gathered round to see Isonash, then disappeared into the crowd as swiftly as they had arrived. Isonash sighed dejectedly, despite having Abenanka and Kiona accompanying him.

"What was that all about?" asked Kiona.

"It's like that every time we travel to Hureatni," her friend described. "Ever since Hasinaw disappeared to be… Well, you know who … Some of the townsfolk here still mistake Isonash for Hasinaw."

"Is their favourite prank *that good*?" Kiona queried.

"Prank? Honesty? It's interchangeable," sighed Isonash again. "My sister is a sensation here. She helped the townsfolk so many times that it's no wonder they praise her more than me. Even Levtiqvah, but that's only because it takes forever for him to understand the language of a man's heart: believe me, I've tried."

"Man or woman, we respect both," Kiona comforted, wrapping her arms around him from behind. "It's true my brother can't get to your heart, but with me, I can. It is my intention to help men like you, not because of your sister or Abenanka, but because you are someone who has been longing for a better appreciation than you already have."

Isonash was stunned to tears. "I… You really *can* understand my heart!"

"Told you that Kiona is special," smiled Abenanka cheerfully.

As a courtesy, the two friends decided to treat Kiona to her own attush, designed by an old friend of theirs. By happy chance, she happened to have one that perfectly reflects Kiona's forest tribe of Shenandoah.

"I made this over seven years ago and, until now, have not found the right person to wear it," the friend told her. "I'm sure you'll take loving care of it. It's the least I can do for you for helping to rescue our children. Thank you."

Kiona was touched. With honour and respect, she wore the attush all the time they were in the town.

Later, as they were tucking into some freshly cooked mahiz, waiting for Hasinaw and Rui-Lin to arrive, their sights of the town were rudely disrupted by the appearance of a group of foreign figures that were clearly out of place.

"Aquilas? What are they doing here? Our land is under Coalition protection!" Abenanka spoke, agitated.

"It's not for the sights and the food; that's for certain," Kiona said warily.

Isonash, who is just as suspicious as Kiona but as highly prepared as Hasinaw in such circumstances, got his sword ready, called an emusi, and calmly approached the intruders.

An elderly man was already confronting the four legionnaires, a centurion, and a commander, whose name is Rufina. Kiona and Abenanka followed their friend until they came face-to-face with their foes. Isonash drew out his emusi defensively. "By what right do you come here?" he demanded.

"This is none of your concern," Commander Rufina responded sternly. "We have been sent by General Glandar on the pursuit of pirates that attacked one of our skyarks off the east coast." Her centurion showed them a refractograph that revealed the culprits they sought.

"I told you, we don't want any trouble here," the elderly man said, drawing out his emusi as an angry crowd gathered to his aid. "If there are any pirates here, then it's up to us and The Coalition to deal with them."

"Those grasps for straws that call themselves The Shepherd's successors?" The commander scoffed rudely. "They're on borrowed time. A stumbling block to those annoying Dragoons who are only delaying the world's answer to a new order."

"Are you threatening us? Because what you say of The Coalition targets all the realms that just want to live in peace with one another," Isonash spoke bluntly. "Their existence helps us to conserve for the next generation."

"Cynthia Caesar is the next generation," Commander Rufina countered ominously. "*We* are the revolution."

"And *we* are the resistance you will one day fear," responded Isonash firmly.

The commander laughed in disbelief at such a suicidal notion, while Isonash stood unmoved and frank. A fifth legionnaire then appeared to inform her that the Coalition had discovered their presence and are on their way to intercept them; so they decided to take their leave.

"I would hate to be in your boots when those words come back to haunt you, finely furnished by red-hot tongs," she spoke lastly before leaving, as outraged Retanians jeered them off. The friends watched as the Aquila's landing barge took off into the sky, just as Hasinaw and Rui-Lin arrived in the town.

"Were those… Aquilas?" Rui-Lin asked.

Hasinaw noticed her brother's emusi and asked him what had happened. Halfway through their conversation, the over-excited people from earlier, recognising Hasinaw at last, gathered round to see her.

And it was thanks to her, Kiona, and the elderly man that they made them appreciate Isonash for bravely standing up against the Aquilas.

Levtiqvah and Hasinaw

It seemed like it had only been yesterday when they arrived in Retania. It is amazing how time flew while Kiona was enjoying the sights of these faraway islands. And when she thought she'd seen only a fraction of this beautiful country, it became apparent that this was the last day before returning with her friends to Gardenia. But just as Kiona was beginning to pack, Hasinaw wanted to show her something so extraordinary that it took her breath away the moment she saw it.

"This is one of the many famous lakes of Retania," Hasinaw said as she revealed it to her. "No matter what time of year it is, with its dense woodland and high mountains, whether in thick snow or a clear sunrise, it always has a special place in my heart."

Kiona quietly strolled forward and seated herself on a boulder, taking in the spectacle of its full majesty. "Levtiqvah was here. I remember this place through him."

"Levtiqvah and I used to spend so much time here," smiled Hasinaw. "We would sit on that very boulder you're sitting on right now, just gazing at the scenery." She sat beside Kiona and looked around, mesmerised by the view. "It truly is wonderful to see this place; to see Retania again with my own eyes."

"You, Hurenitay, Abenanka, and Princess Roso were the only ones he'd met who fully understood him," Kiona addressed.

"And, evidently, only once Abenanka, my brother and I became part of The Father's family," clarified Hasinaw as she gently embraced her. "Being with you, it's as if he never left me. Do you remember, through his memories, the time he gave me a white sweet cherry blossom?"

"I do indeed," answered Kiona. "You discovered the gift he left on your bunk in the Kimuyay Garrison when The Shepherds existed."

"Right. I spent the entire day trying to find out who left me that flower," Hasinaw remembered.

"I talked to all the men I knew, but they all denied any knowledge. It was a mystery," she continued, "until later that evening when I was alone. Levtiqvah appeared in my barracks, and when I told him about the white sweet cherry blossom, he confessed that he was the one who had left it. Although... He couldn't adequately express his true feelings and instead had to apologise… And as I studied The Father's words, I gained a deeper understanding of his situation. He is, after all, an angel who's pure, and I'm a woman who's not. Being romantically together would only make him impure and result in me giving birth to an unnatural and uncontrollable giant, just like what happened to his brothers that fell long ago.

"No one would think that he is fully grown and suffers misjudgement. He was so forlorn, he told me, because The Father had separated him from the angel he was the heart to in order to fulfil a specific purpose. From the very moment I first had him within my chest, I can tell that he is a very special element to our hearts. Being separated had, for fifteen years, made him feel lost, longingly seeking to be whole with his proprietor again. And it was only after he became one with your heart after he died as Achak, did the name Tiqvah come into my recollection."

"I can so totally relate with him," Kiona described, "as we were incarnated separately to bring forth The Maid of the Heart I've become. My heart couldn't be happier to be where he belongs now, and, although he can't be with you anymore physically, he can still cherish you spiritually whenever I allow him to visit you." She hugged her, sharing the experience from Levtiqvah, as their hearts pressed together.

"You know," smiled Hasinaw. "Since he became one with your heart, the love that Levtiqvah and I had for each other has certainly morphed ours into a powerful friendship."

"Save your love for The Father and his Son," responded Kiona happily. "They will appreciate it more."

Hasinaw chortled fondly. "Like brother, like sister. Just as he was and still is, that angel is a real stickler. Not always succeeding but always striving, just as we're striving to serve the one who truly saved our souls from our own destruction. If ever there is a good example of The Father's angels, he's it."

The two friends continued their last view of the lake before returning to the cise to finish packing.

But as the friends arrived in the evening at the Kimuyay Garrison, with gentle snowflakes falling from the sky once more, they all had to bid a fond farewell to Hasinaw before she embarked on a different skyark, retiring to Austrinia, where her family is in a hidden location.

"Thank you for telling me more about yourself and Levtiqvah, Hasinaw," smiled Kiona before turning to her brother. "I still wish I had enough time to learn more about you, though, Isonash."

"It's not as if I'm going away anytime soon, Kiona," Isonash laughed. "After transferring from Castellan to Gardenia, it is to be my home for a long while yet, so there's plenty of time for us to get to know each other."

"And hopefully, next time we meet," hinted Hasinaw, "it will be when Gardenia is in its time of Cold Nights, and I'll be competing for the Tundra Talisman in Kocoum."

"We'll be cheering for you when that day comes," beamed Kiona as the two gave each other one farewell hug.

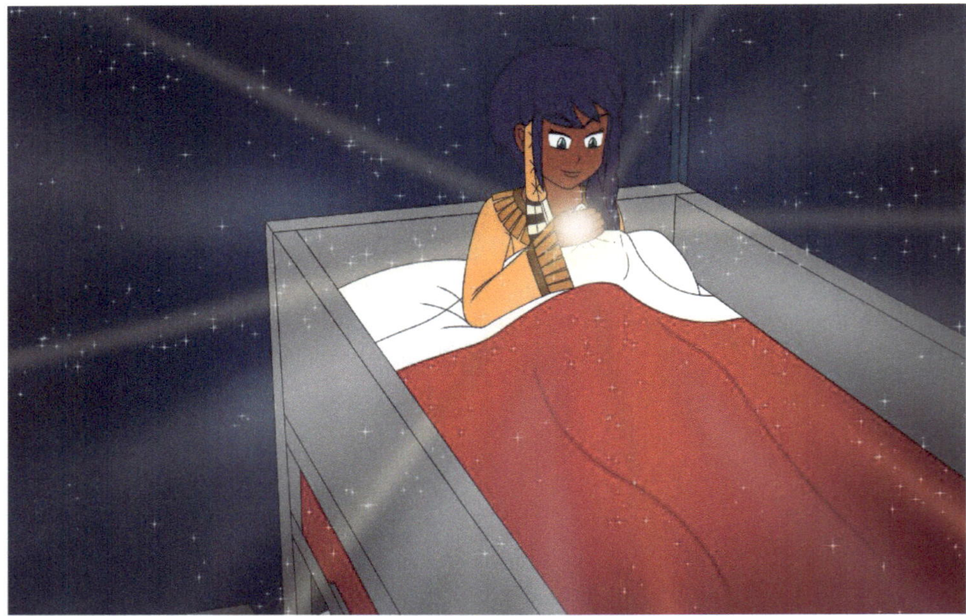

The red sun slowly set in the west, and Hasinaw was long gone when their skyark arrived to take the tired friends back to Gardenia. They were exhausted after their long day and retired to the traveller's bunks. Kiona shared her bunk with Abenanka, and for a while, the two had a warming conversation about their time in Retania and Levtiqvah's involvement in Abenanka's life.

Long afterwards, Abenanka was sound asleep in her bunk, and while Kiona was making herself comfortable in hers, and after a long prayer, she still had one more person to talk to.

"Well, Levtiqvah, you certainly had quite a time with Hasinaw, Isonash, and Abenanka, didn't you?" she whispered while clenching the gentle glow of her heart. "Your memories are helping me to understand you during our time apart, our friends, and who I need to be now as The Maid of the Heart. I know this flesh is not as pure as my already saved soul, but with your help to restrain it from any temptations, I can at least strive to serve The Father's Son, just as I did before being incarnated as Kiona."

She happily snuggled into her pillow and, in no time, had caught up with Abenanka in joyful sleep, her heart acting as their comforting nightlight.

Titles from

1: Kiona the Gardenian

2: The Maid of the Heart

3: Rubecula & Nascha

4: The Tree of Agape

5: A Zephyr Before The Tempest

6: The Passion of Kiona

7: Abigail & Rui-Lin

8: Come Full Circle